Help keep the countryside tidy by taking your rubbish home with you. If you are out and about and see rubbish lying around, tell a grown-up about it right away!

Ducks, swans and geese need their greens, just like you! Bread is like junk food for birds - it fills them up but isn't very good for them! Instead give them food they'll really enjoy, like peas, corn or bird seed.

Don't pick the flowers, they should stay in the ground for the bees and birds to enjoy.

THIS AUTUMN BOOK BELONGS TO:

....

Autumn
Publishing

Published in 2019
by Igloo Books Ltd
Cottage Farm
Sywell
NN6 0BJ
www.igloobooks.com

Autumn is an imprint of Bonnier Books UK

Illustrated by Sebastien Braun
Designed by Steve Prosser
Written by Claire Mowat

GUA009 0419
2 4 6 8 10 9 7 5 3 1
ISBN 978-1-78905-269-5

Printed and manufactured in China

RSPCA

Buttercup
Farm
Friends

BEST OF
FRIENDS

Autumn
Publishing

Best friends Rufus and Ruby are different in every way.

Kitten Ruby
is shy...

... but puppy
Rufus loves
to play.

Rufus is full of energy and he loves to have fun.

So now he needs a bigger home with somewhere nice to run.

VROOM!!

Poor Ruby wasn't wanted and was left to be found.

She felt very scared and didn't dare make a sound.

When Ruby was rescued, she felt frightened and ran to hide.

Rufus looks after
her and now he never
leaves her side.

Soon Rufus
and Ruby…

… find a new
home they
can share.

They both feel so lucky that they can stay as a pair.

They are going to live on Buttercup Farm...

... and Rufus can't wait to explore.

But Ruby is nervous. She's never seen a cow before!

Daisy the cow startles Ruby with a loud, 'Moo!'

She wants to tell Ruby, "It's nice to meet you."

Seymour the fox says,
'Hello', but now he
wants to sleep.

BAA!!

Then they hear a 'Baa' and go to meet Lucy the sheep.

Now Rufus
and Ruby
meet Reggie
the badger...

CLUCK!!

... and a loud
'cluck' means
they've met
Hetty the hen.

QUACK!

Dilly the duck splashes in the pond…

… while muddy Penelope the pig plays in her pen.

Now Rufus and Ruby will never be alone.

On Buttercup Farm, they've found their forever home.